Caffeine Ni

CW00401287

THE WINDSOR CURIOSITY

~STEAM, SMOKE & MIRRORS~

A Steam, Smoke & Mirrors Short Story

Colin Edmonds

Further insights and extracts from the secret journals

of

Professor Artemus More PhD (Cantab) FRS

Fiction aimed at the heart
and the head…

Published by Caffeine Nights Publishing 2017

Copyright © Colin Edmonds 2017

Colin Edmonds has asserted his right under the Copyright, Designs
and Patents Act 1998 to be identified as the author of this work.

CONDITIONS OF SALE

ISBN: 9781973559306

Published in Great Britain by

Caffeine Nights Publishing

4 Eton Close

Walderslade

Chatham

Kent

ME5 9AT

caffeinenights.com

steamsmokeandmirrors.com

Everything else by

Default, Luck and Accident

THE WINDSOR

CURIOSITY

The plot was to kill Queen Victoria.

And why not? Back in 1882, Her Majesty herself admitted, "It is worth being shot at to see how much one is loved."

Not that she had any great affection for the idea of regicide per se, of course, but being a pragmatic Monarch she understood that the sound of gunfire in her immediate vicinity was not without its advantages. And with so much ordnance discharged in her name over the last sixty-two years, probably felt it only fair she took a few rounds in return.

So far, there had been seven attempts on Victoria's life, all failures, obviously, and each of them while Her Majesty rode in an open carriage. But only six were point-blank albeit boss-eyed shootings. The other was made by a hunchback called John William Bean who, unable to shoot her because he forgot to bring a pistol, had to resort to jumping up and trying to whack the old Queen with a walking stick. Such was his success, no wounds were inflicted, and after a nifty reshape even her bonnet appeared unscathed by the battering.

Here and now, in 1899, with the Queen aged seventy-nine and starting to feel every year of it, the visit from the estimable Superintendent William Melville bearing a summons from Her Majesty came as somewhat of a surprise. In his capacity as head of the Special Branch of the Metropolitan Police, he invited my stage magicians: the thirty-year old dark haired, handsome American, Michael Magister and his very lovely, very English twenty-one-year-old auburn-tressed associate Phoebe Le Breton, to perform a gentle programme of their most brutal, gut-wrenching illusions for the jollification of Her Majesty at Windsor Castle. Naturally, Michael and Phoebe understood the word 'invitation' to mean 'forceful, arm-twisting command'.

This immediately raised several eyebrows, not least because The Special Branch was usually tasked with foiling treachery by the nation's enemies, not booking the entertainment for a Royal performance. Yes, Michael and Phoebe were remarkable magicians, crowd-pleasing stars of the Music Hall, so the engagement made some sense. But, more importantly, Michael and Phoebe were no strangers to dealing with the courageous and heavily moustached Superintendent Melville. You see, he frequently, albeit reluctantly, sought their assistance. Well, as professional mystifiers steeped in the noble arts of deception and lies, they could provide a specialised insight into the more esoteric crimes which were now baffling the finest minds at Scotland Yard on a horribly regular basis. The world was now officially going mad, and Melville needed help from those who could make sense of the insanity.

And he could hardly deny my magicians' success. Since their secondment as Crime Consultants to Her Majesty's Special Branch, Michael Magister and Phoebe Le Breton had successfully resolved: 'The Arcane Mystery of the Mind-Bending Music Hall Murderer' and were well on the way to solving 'The Very Esoteric Oscar Wilde Portrait of Eternal Youth Poser', and "The Really Quite Bat-shit Bonkers Man's Arm Lodged in The Side Door of The Bank of England Conundrum' – if you'll kindly forgive the expression Conundrum.

(By the way, exaggerated accounts of these nail-biting investigations can be found in my personal files: "Steam, Smoke & Mirrors" also known as "The Mesmer Curiosity", and "Steam, Smoke & Mirrors 2: The Lazarus Curiosity", all published by Caffeine Nights)

So, naturally, Michael and Phoebe happily agreed to perform for a much-loved old Queen at Windsor Castle; Michael motivated by his awe of Her Majesty and to further his ambition of becoming the first American to be knighted for simply being famous; and Phoebe out of sheer cussed devilment and her flagrant disregard of the Establishment.

Additionally, they knew that in making such an unusual request, the honourable Monarch and the honest to goodness Melville were very clearly up to something doubtful. 'Dubiosity' Michael called it. He possessed not just an uncanny ability to misuse the English language, but also ab instinct for sniffing out skulduggery, while Phoebe was simply suspicious of anything or anyone in authority.

And so, with those altruistic justifications borne in mind, I made the financially heart-breaking decision to cancel tonight's late performance at the Metropolitan Theatre of Steam, Smoke and Mirrors in London's Edgware Road. With the help of Wicko the dwarf, my stoic and workshy associate, we loaded what was needed aboard the Steam-Wagon and chugged west to countrified Berkshire and Windsor Castle.

The opportunity was far too glorious to overlook. There was irony in assassinating the Queen in the comfort and security of her own home. And the publicity? It would be worldwide. At the very least!

All of which is why and how Michael Magister: The Industrial Age Illusionist, and Phoebe Le Breton: the Queen of Steam and Goddess of the Aethyr, found themselves setting up the gruesome equipment with which they planned to enthral and mystify the royal assembly; quaintly titled illusions: "The Iron Maiden of Agonised Doom" and "The Coffin of Death" (is there any other kind?) and delicate props such as "The Scimitar of Dismemberment" and "The Pulsa Pistol of Explosive Fury". All within the elegant, rarefied confines of Windsor Castle's Green Drawing Room.

By the way, the Green Drawing Room is so called because it is a drawing room with green coloured furniture and wall coverings. Remarkably unimaginative you might think, but incredibly logical for helping newer footmen while they got their bearings. Except for those sadly afflicted with colour blindness, of course, who still wandered about the Castle corridors scratching their heads.

Tonight's Green Drawing Room venue was an intriguing departure from the norm. Castle performances were usually staged in the larger Waterloo Room. Named, Michael suspected, purely to get up the nose of any visiting dignitary from across the Channel.

Of course, there would be no objection concerning this move to a smaller venue. The magic show would benefit from the greater intimacy – making it so much easier to snuff out the life of Queen Victoria.

"That's an oil painting by Laurits Tuxen," said Phoebe, pointing to the six feet wide canvas hanging on the wall, nearby. "If you look closely, it features all the Queen's extended family, children, children-in-law and grandchildren, all set in this very room."

Michael took a pause from testing the sharpness of the spikes on the Iron Maiden, licked the bubble of blood from his thumb and squinted up at the canvas. By the way, do try and get to see this picture for yourself, it is not only remarkable for the accuracy of its portraits, but also a significant historical document. "Pheebs, I don't see you in this gathering."

"Michael, if Tuxen had been compelled to include all the Prince of Wales's children, legitimate or otherwise, the painting would be wider than the Bayeux Tapestry!" Phoebe lifted the lid of the highly polished metallised Coffin of Death, testing the - HISHHHT! - gasp of blue smoke. "Apparently, it proved rather difficult to compose the picture, with rival Dukes and Princesses refusing to be seen next to one another. And who would want to stand beside to me?"

Michael shrugged and nodded. "Even *I* get paid to."

"Beast!"

The spinning topper Phoebe flung missed his head by inches. Even as he ducked Michael knew it was wrong. The hat glanced a delicate Chinese Qianlong Period vase, causing it to wobble and then topple from the sideboard. Time seemed to slow while Phoebe watched the eighteenth-century Buddhist Temple antique tumble gracefully before shattering in a shower of colourful but worthless cloisonné enamel … until Michael spun and caught the beauty, two-handed just before it hit the carpet.

"Well held," said Superintendent William Melville, quietly from the doorway. If he in any way shared Phoebe's relief, his blue eyes did not betray it. "Miss Le Breton, Mr. Magister. The seating arrangements have been approved and Her Majesty's guests are assembling outside."

It would not matter who sat where. No. In these intimate surroundings one could murder the Queen from any angle.

The three rows of chairs arced gently around the performance area. In the centre of the front row, Her Majesty, flanked by The Munshi, her turbaned manservant, and Sir Arthur Bigge, her small but modestly named Private Secretary. Others approved to share the ring-side view were Melville's superior, Sir Cumberland Sinclair, the slender, genial and utterly inept Special Branch Assistant Commissioner; Lord Scortum, the Queen's grey whiskered adjutant, frequently referred to in court circulars as 'the well-known spelling error'; the rotund, nervous-lest-he-put-a-foot-wrong Sir Maudsley Spillage, the Member of Parliament in the Constituency of Greater Windsor, recently elected on a popular local platform of patriotic anti-Republicanism; Superintendent Melville and then Wicko. Yes, our disgruntled associate would sit there scowling at the end of the front row, poised, ready and hiding the Pulsa Pistol of Explosive Fury. Occupying the seats behind, ranks of sniffy castle officials; then right at the back, suitably grateful servants. None among the thirty-strong audience was remotely aware that our grim-faced dwarf was in possession of a concealed murderous weapon.

As for myself, I would lurk in my usual anonymity at the back of the room, observing the performance and adjusting the lights. Oh, me? I am Professor Artemus More. Some consider me a 'mad scientist'. Mad? Well, occasionally. The rest of the time I'm just quietly furious. I prefer to think of myself more modestly as an inventor, visionary, and genius. Oh, and producer of the theatre's magical performances. It was I who taught Michael the benefits of modesty. I am also the complete and utter epitome of discretion.

But between you and me, the most notable absentee from this evening's proceedings? His Majesty the Prince of Wales, who was apparently claiming a prior engagement. Yes. In the boudoir of either Mrs Langtry or Mrs Keppel. It could also be safely assumed by the few who knew the secret, that the heir to the throne had not been exactly thrilled by the prospect of having to watch one of his illegitimate daughters performing on the stage before his mother. Oh. Have I said too much?

Michael and Phoebe now waited, pulses pumping, behind the draped, makeshift curtain: he, elegant in a frothy shirt, golden metallised waistcoat, black trousers and cravat; she in her long, deep red, basque-tied, tight-waisted dress, slit to almost reveal too much thigh. The rich colour of her costume in perfect harmony with her low- slung earrings and the striking blood-red ruby ring she wore upon the middle finger of her right hand.

My magicians pulled nervous faces at one another when they heard the audience rise and politely applaud as the Queen made her entrance; plump in black mourning lace, and slumped in her bath chair, pushed by the tall, imposing Abdul Karim, the much frowned-upon Munshi. I liked the man, but the royal hangers-on bitterly resented Her Majesty's Indian personal servant far more than they ever did her late, Scottish personal servant John Brown. And they all positively hated him!

With the monarch gently manoeuvred into the gap in the front row, I dimmed the lights, commencing the Steam, Smoke & Mirrors Royal Programme of Magical Illusions.

It was all falling into place. Tonight, history would be made. The loathsome Queen would rule no more.

The show began well, both Michael and Phoebe were in fine form; their opening patter sharp and witty, while the audience remained sour faced and unamused. Admittedly, those towards the back were rather enjoying the performance, but felt it wasn't their place to express that enjoyment. In fact, the front two rows frowned at Michael's reference to the recent electoral success of Sir Maudsley Spillage. "He said in one of his most stirring anti-opposition speeches, 'For years, they lied to you. For years, they cheated you. For years, they stole from you. Now give *me* a chance'."

Suddenly the Queen let slip a titter, and Sir Maudsley Spillage took that as his cue to fake a grin and nod like a happy stallion, and then the rest of the crowd agreed they had official permission to enjoy the joke as well.

Her Majesty also responded favourably to the opening gambit: the Queen's chosen card (the Queen of Hearts, yes, it was a bit of Magister 'Old Madam', but it might help towards the knighthood) disappearing from the deck, then Michael magically finding the self-same card hidden within the silken folds of the Munshi's headdress.

Abdul Karin looked suitably surprised.

"Bravo, Mr. Magister," whispered the Queen.

Sir Cumberland Sinclair gasped at the audacity, holding the back of his hand to his mouth in amazement. Sir Arthur Bigge shuffled in discomfort. Lord Scortum scoffed "Dang me breeches!" whatever the hell that meant. Sir Maudsley Spillage again grinned and nodded, which seemed to be what he did, while Wicko swallowed nervously. Superintendent Melville quietly noted the reactions of the dignitaries and those of the household staff sitting behind.

Of course, none of them remotely suspected that the Queen, and The Munshi were mischievously, happily complicit in a little pre-show duplicity.

Those of you familiar with my first memoir will recall that before seconding Michael and Phoebe to the Special Branch, Melville had to seek Royal approval; and at their meeting Victoria was found to be admiring of her spirited granddaughter and amused by the Magister.

Following polite applause, the impressive, upright "Iron Maiden of Agonised Doom" was trundled into view and Michael displayed proud and clear the rows of sharp silver skewers poking out from the open door. That the vicious spikes were too short and the Maiden deceptively too deep to cause any kind of Doom, Agonised or otherwise, was curiously never admitted during his otherwise detailed demonstration.

The Goddess Phoebe then having enchanted Michael with her seductive 'fluence, bound and bundled him into the Maiden and to the alarm of the crowd and hideous cries from Michael, dramatically SCHTOOOM! slammed shut the lid!

As you now know, there was quite enough space between the spikes and the certain death for Michael to slip his easily removable bonds, exit from the false panel at the rear and out into the dark-light.

When Phoebe, with a FLUMPH! of purple smoke and flash of white light threw open the lid, Michael was seen to be gone … only then to be heard from behind the audience shouting, "Not this time, Goddess!"

Heads turned, gasps followed and polite clapping ensued. You'll find in a space as relatively confined as the Green Drawing Room, that a puff of smoke and a low intensity flash is quite sufficient to disorient the gathering, certainly long enough for Michael to scramble silently past and into position.

Good. The performance was engaging these fools. Soon. Soon.

Now it was the turn of the apparently emboldened Magister to resist the Goddess's enticement, turn the tables and lure her into "The Coffin of Death"!

Locked within the supposedly cast iron coffer, Phoebe summoned all her supple dexterity to quickly curl and tuck herself into a ball at one end of the coffin, timed perfectly, just moments before Magister sliced the casket into three equal parts with easy strokes from the diabolical, fire-edged 'Scimitar of Dismemberment'. The severed sections were separated, wheeled about with merciless abandon, then re-joined as one solid piece, while the audience thrummed with alarm.

But when the lid of 'The Coffin of Death' was raised and The Goddess arose alive, and lovely, the audience expressed their relief with approval.

Excellent. The audience was now utterly enthralled. The time was right. To strike the old Queen down.

"Your Majesty, ladies and gentlemen," declaimed Michael. "Our finale tonight is a salute. A tip of the top hat to a stunning illusion practised only by skilled magicians who studied under a great guru, the very ridiculously named Abbah-Ra-Kadabra. Yes, this is a dice with death known by lesser adepts as 'Catching A Bullet In The Teeth'. And I know I don't need to describe what happens in this illusion because everything you need is pretty much there in the title!"

Michael gazed along the front row. Where we come from, Michael and I would call this a tough crowd. The ringsiders sitting there knitting by the guillotine. The Queen nodded her ascent. The

Munshi looked imperious. Sir Arthur Bigge was still to turn a sneer into a smile. Sir Cumberland Sinclair beamed broadly, rubbing his hands together as he was wont to do when excited by danger which didn't involve him. Sir Maudsley Spillage cracked a sheepish grin. Melville was as calm as ever. Wicko stroked a nervous bead of sweat from his top lip as he reached inside his jacket for the locked strong box containing the weapon.

Phoebe stepped forward to continue the narrative, "But tonight, we shall take that illusion to a new dimension of danger. Tonight, the Magister will perform 'Catching The Pulse of Energised Aethyr In The Mouth'!"

"Damnable mouthful," scoffed Lord Scortum. All he'd done all night was scoff, that one.

With a dramatic gesture, Phoebe summoned Wicko. "Behold, we present to you the most formidable weapon in the world – The Pulsatronic Pistol"

Wicko stood and, resting the metal strong box upon upturned palms, approached the performance area with imperious reverence, then he stopped and turned to face the audience. Phoebe held aloft an ornate golden key, KERLACK! unlocked the box, HIISSSST! hinged open the lid and held aloft…

"Your Majesty, ladies and gentlemen, we present for you: The Pulsatronic Pistol!"

It was a weapon of disturbing, but lavish beauty (of course it was, I designed it!), forged in the shape of a Smith & Wesson revolver, but that's where any similarity finished. Bronze in colour; the revolving cylinder solid, not a single hole bored for bullets; thin copper piping snaked about the barrel then served an array of fine-tooth cogs. The carved grip was of highly polished dark mahogany, inlaid with elaborate brass detail.

The audience murmured in both admiration and apprehension. Melville sat up. Finally! He had briefly seen the Pulsa, or one very much like it, used in that attempt on the life of the Prime Minister; right outside the Metropolitan Theatre of Steam, Smoke and Mirrors. The attempt foiled by Michael and Phoebe.

Wicko bowed and returned to his seat.

Michael then explained with such confidence, it sounded like he knew what he was talking about. Which he didn't. "The Pulsa does not discharge modern bullets or cartridges or shot. A single pull of the trigger spins the chamber. The coils within generate a ball of explosive energy culled from the very atmosphere we breathe, energy the Goddess calls the Aethyr. And Phoebe, alone can tame that energy, and compel the force to submit to her will. As she is about to demonstrate."

"Observe," ordered Phoebe. "At your collective peril."

She pulled the trigger. The cogs turned and the chamber started a lazy spin. Then faster. Faster. Finally emitting a low pitched WHUUUUM!

"Now. With the charge of Aethyr generated. History is about to be made. A second pull of the trigger will discharge the sphere of destructive energy directly at …. the target … of … my choice!"

Phoebe swung the Pulsa, aimed and pulled the trigger. Instantly a ball of white energy spat from the barrel, speeding across the room trailing a tracer of mauve and exploded into its target: Michael's top hat, placed atop the "Coffin of Death". The flare of purple flame reduced the topper to glowing, floating embers.

Michael and Phoebe both turned to face their audience, arms held high in dramatic pose, Phoebe still gripping the Pulsa. The silence was stark, almost shocked. The Queen remained impassive. The crowd stunned, wide-eyed, trying to process the significance of what they had just witnessed. And the astonishing destructive power of the Pulsa.

"Hold the pose," Michael whispered to Phoebe. "Be brave. Make them have it."

Then Victoria gave a wave of endorsement. The audience breathed and broke into uncertain applause. Once again, if the Queen approved, well, so must they.

"Your Majesty, ladies and gentlemen, you need not be cowed by the power of the Aethyr," ordered Phoebe. "For now, it is only the Magister who should be afraid."

Again, Michael took up the story. "Because tonight, for the first time, and, possibly the last, I will attempt to catch a ball of that destructive, energised Aethyr … in my mouth."

The audience mumbled with great unease. Concerned expressions filled the air. "The man's mad!", "Dang me Breeches!", "American fool!" and "He looks stupid enough to try it!" None of it remotely reassuring.

"'The man's mad', somebody said," said Michael. "Which I would add was the kindest remark! Am I mad? Let's find out. I will now respectfully invite the Goddess to take her mark."

Phoebe slunk with trademark sensuality to her firing position.

"To remind you all, once again. Phoebe will pull the trigger to generate the charge. It is the second pull of the trigger which fires the Aethyr – the very ball of energy I will catch in my mouth. But should I fail, I hereby declare before you all that I absolve Phoebe, the Queen of Steam and Goddess of the Aethyr of all responsibility. And if he'll forgive the scorch marks, I bequeath my golden cravat to Mister M. By which I mean Superintendent Melville." Melville did not appear entirely thrilled at the thought. "May I now ask for total silence? Oh, I see I already have it."

Michael adopted a pose of firm concentration. Knees slightly bent. Eyes closed. Deep, controlled breathing. The seconds ticked. All eyes flashed between Michael and Phoebe. I dimmed the lights once again. The temperature rose. The tension all but palpable.

"Goddess. Please. Charge the Pulsa!"

Phoebe pulled the trigger. The silence was broken by the WHUUUUM of the weapon.

"Take aim!"

Phoebe raised the Pulsa into the firing position. Directly at Michael's face. No more than ten feet away.

Seize the moment! Now!!

Then there was a noise. A chair. She barely saw the shadow-figure that sent her sprawling her dazed, tumbling to the floor. The weapon fell from her grip. The man grabbed the charged Pulsa. WHUUUM! Levelled the barrel directly at the Queen and screamed: "A message from the Black Bishop! Die, you blasphemous witch!"

With his face contorted with hatred, Sir Maudsley Spillage pulled the trigger. The crowd screamed and cowered. Melville and the Munshi dived to cover Victoria with their bodies and...

Nothing.

Spillage took a step closer. Yanked the trigger again.

"Die, bitch Queen! Die!"

Again - nothing.

"Gah!!" Spillage raised the Pulsa to smash it down on the Queen's skull, before he was hit by a bull. Bundled to one side. He fell with his assailant in a tangle of arms and legs.

In the chaos of screaming, shouting and scrambling to escape, Spillage, insane with rage, lashed out at his attacker with fists and knees and Michael recoiled, mouth bloodied.

The traitorous MP struggled to his feet. Then Melville and Phoebe dragged him down again. Phoebe gripped his neck between her thighs as Melville punched him in the groin, before forcing both arms together and snapping shut the handcuffs.

"Can't breathe…" gasped Spillage, his face obscured within Phoebe's dress, his nose crushed by her scissors lock.

"Oh, quit moaning," said Michael, wiping his lip on a silk white handkerchief. "I know men who'd pay good money to be in that position!"

"Chance would be a fine thing!" said Phoebe.

Oddly enough, that was the last thing Michael remembered before he bravely fainted clean away.

When the Industrial Age Illusionist finally recovered most of his senses, he found himself sitting on the carpet, propped up against the "Coffin of Death" with Phoebe dabbing his split lip and assuring him no teeth were broken. The Green Drawing Room was empty, save for the magicians, Wicko and me. The illusions were intact but the Pulsa Pistol was gone. Swept up by

Melville. Determined to understand the technology. Ha. He should proceed with caution. It will smoulder in self-destruction as soon as his ham-fisted Scotland Yard associates start their tampering. I knew this world was not yet ready for the Pulsa.

As Wicko and I began preparing the Iron Maiden for the journey back to the theatre, Superintendent Melville strode into the chamber with confidence and purpose. "Her Majesty remains composed and untroubled by the attempt on her life. Naturally, the royal officials are furious, but when are they not?"

"Your plan worked," said Michael, which with his swollen lip sounded more like, "More pla mert."

"Indeed," said Melville, gently.

It seems that some weeks before, the Superintendent had acquired the knowledge that a traitor wedded to the destruction of the Monarchy and advocating return to Catholicism, a disciple of the enigmatic Black Bishop, had inveigled himself into a position of trust. Suspicion fell upon the patriotic highly popular Member of Parliament. But Melville could not be certain. Lord Scortum was suddenly showing strange signs of disgruntlement.

Melville needed to supply the traitor with a glorious opportunity and the magic show was a perfect trap. It would be made known that every one of the invited audience would be routinely searched for any kind of murdering tool, except the magicians and their props. And their performance comprised of nothing more than a collection of instruments of death. Michael Magister and Phoebe Le Breton would effectively become the traitor's personal armourers – and he was spoilt for choice.

Yes, Michael and Phoebe suspected Melville's motives for arranging the royal performance, but to what end? Only the Queen and the Munshi were complicit in his plot.

"In which case, Mister M, you flew pretty close to the wind tonight. You had no idea the Pulsa wouldn't fire."

"We were fortunate," nodded Melville. "I fully expected the traitor to seize his opportunity with the sword."

"The Scimitar of Dismemberment," corrected Phoebe.

Melville ignored the comment saying: "Spillage was fleet of foot. Far quicker than a man of his size has any right to be. But then, mercifully, your pistol failed to function," admitted Melville.

"Mercifully it did," said Phoebe.

Her tone was enough to sow a seed of doubt. Was the misfire an accident? He would never know for certain.

"Your performance this evening has not been found wanting. And praise for the greatest possible courage must go…"

"Please, Mister M. We're just happy to help," said Michael, holding up a modest hand.

"...to Her Majesty," Melville continued, "who played her part with nerves of tempered steel. Well, then. I bid you both goodnight."

Michael licked his stinging lip. "Even from where we stood, Pheebs and I had Spillage nailed as one you couldn't trust."

"Ah. Your unfailing instinct, no doubt," said Melville, wryly, walking away.

"No. Because he was a politician," said Phoebe.

"What's going to happen with Spillage now?" wondered Michael.

"Our fish is hooked and netted, Mr. Magister. How he is filleted, is beyond my remit."

Phoebe piped up, her eyes narrow. "What happened here tonight. It will never be reported will it...?"

Melville stopped. Looked around the Green Drawing Room of Windsor Castle. At the scattered chairs. At Michael's blood stain on the carpet.

"Miss Le Breton ... nothing happened here tonight."

And with that, the head of The Special Branch turned and left.

THE END

Queen Victoria was a huge admirer of conjuring and the work of magicians. She invited the Godfather of magic, Robert-Houdin, to perform at Buckingham Palace back in 1848. Five years later the great man was asked to return to entertain at a children's party for Victoria's daughter, Princess Louise. In 1849, John Henry Anderson 'The Great Wizard of the North' was summoned to entertain Victoria at Balmoral, as was the American magician Harry Kellar in 1880.

Curiously, the record books make no mention of 1899 and the royal performance of Michael Magister and Phoebe Le Breton at Windsor Castle.

WHY DID THE PULSATRONIC PISTOL NOT FIRE?

Ah. Well. You see, Sir Maudsley Spillage MP and, indeed, Superintendent Melville could not know the grip on the Pulsa is moulded to accommodate Phoebe's ruby ring. The jewel slots into the aperture precisely carved into the handle. Whoever wears the ruby can shoot the Pulsa. No ring, no fire power. It was never going to be Sir Maudsley's   night.

If you enjoyed this Steam, Smoke and Mirrors short story featuring Michael Magister and Phoebe Le Breton why not try one of the great steampunk Steam, Smoke and Mirrors novels by Colin Edmonds:

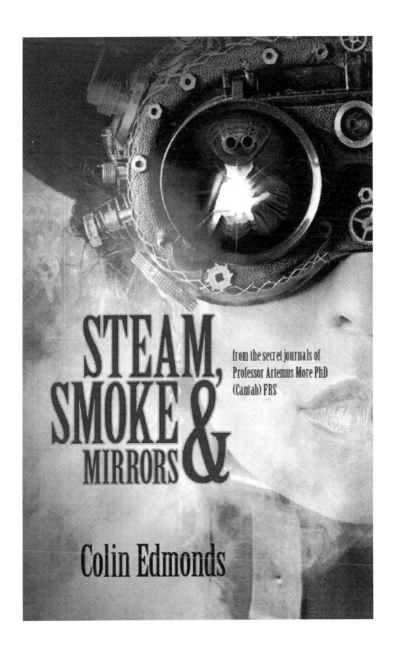

STEAM, SMOKE & MIRRORS

from the secret journals of
Professor Artemus More PhD
(Cantab) FRS

Colin Edmonds

Steam Smoke & Mirrors Volume 1 –

The Mesmer Curiosity

STEAM, SMOKE & MIRRORS

from the secret journals of

Professor Artemus More PhD (Cantab) FRS

by Colin Edmonds

When a Music Hall hypnotist escapes from the London County Asylum she leaves a single word on the wall of her cell - scrawled in blood: 'MAGISTER'. Terror then stalks the capital's streets as the killing spree begins. But why does Superintendent William Melville of The Special Branch call upon the skills of brilliant stage magician Michael Magister and his glamorous assistant Phoebe Le Breton to help capture the murderer? Especially as Michael is one of those named on the death list.

From the recently discovered journals of Professor Artemus More, secrets are laid bare, mysteries revealed, illusions exposed and conspiracies uncovered, all in a Steampunk vision of Victorian Britain. But is anything truly what it seems?

Or is it all just Steam, Smoke and Mirrors?

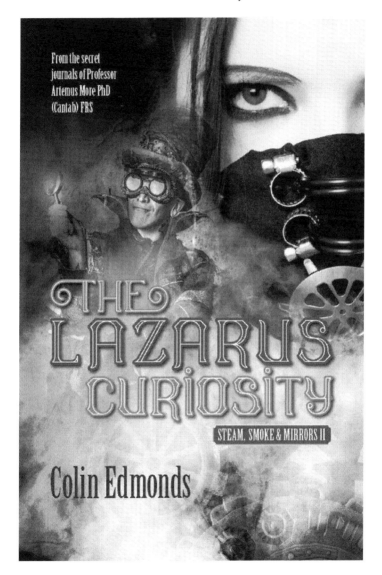

From the secret
journals of Professor
Artemus More PhD
(Cantab) FRS

THE LAZARUS CURIOSITY

STEAM, SMOKE & MIRRORS II

Colin Edmonds

BAFFLED by a severed arm, dangling from the centre of a locked door in the Bank of England…

PANICKED by a satanic portrait painter, determined to disgrace the Royal family…

TERRORISED by a deadly gas, primed to wipe out the Government…

With great reluctance, what else can Superintendent William Melville of the Special Branch do but, once again, send for … THE MAGICIANS!

When not performing two sold-out shows every night, Music Hall Steampunk illusionists and consultants to Scotland Yard, slick-talking Michael Magister and the feisty Phoebe Le Breton, must solve the crime of the century, while saving the nation from a conclave of fiendish psychopaths led by the crazed renegade Jesuit known only as 'The Black Bishop'.

In the sequel to their acclaimed debut in 'Steam, Smoke & Mirrors', who dare Michael and

Phoebe trust in this dark Victorian world of weird science, conspiracy and the occult?

Murder and malevolence, treachery and tragedy – all must surely be inevitable!

Especially when the Tarot predicts – DEATH.

Coming soon

Read an exclusive extract from the next Steam,
Smoke & Mirrors novel: Nostradamus Curiosity

Steam, Smoke & Mirrors 3

THE NOSTRADAMUS CURIOSITY

1.

Yes. Michael Magister, the Industrial Age Illusionist, had died. His face, hands and the best part of both his lungs perished in a caustic cloud of yellow Brimstone; the merciless vapour confected by man purely, though purity had little to do with it, for the sole purpose of destroying his fellow man.

It was in the nave of Westminster Abbey, in an extraordinarily uncharacteristic display of courage, that Michael saved the craven lives of almost all the ruling elite, who naturally could hardly wait to demonstrate their ingratitude!

Wicko, my brilliant dwarf confederate, was only too aware of the monumental fire-storm that was about careening our way faster than a Coney Island roller coaster. And the fault was mine.

You see, Michael's manic urgency, and naturally misguided decency, to thwart such an international outrage was so earnestly convincing, I allowed us to expose ourselves. I let 'altruism' trump our survival instinct of 'all-false-ism'. Yes, I know it is not a proper expression, but needs must. The existence of 'The Ferrous Dodo', our compact, highly advanced dirigible, a secret we guarded for so long, had now been revealed.

Despite the dusky gloom, hundreds of witnesses in the streets surrounding Parliament and Westminster Abbey shouted and screamed and tried to control their horses as they watched our silver-skinned airship sweep around the clock tower of Big Ben three hundred feet above the Thames, before coming about and descending quickly to a shuddering turf-churning halt on the stretch of Green beside the Abbey's north door. The slack-jawed throng then watched a stylish man and a stunning woman jump down from a door in the belly of the beast and sprint to the north door of the great gothic edifice.

Most maintained a cautious distance, alarmed by the malevolent moan which resonated from the idling engine of the mysterious sky ship. Others, more curious, came for a closer look, daring to poke and stroke the metal skin, although their reward was a sharp, jolting crack of static. Then, from within the Abbey came a loud and terrible commotion. Panicked government officials, arms a-flailing, spewed out with unedifying haste, fighting and bundling aboard their carriages. The woman supervised the loading of a prostrate body aboard the silver ovoid which promptly lifted from the ground and, with an ear-piercing whine, swung its nose to the west and took to the sky in breath-taking haste.

Some in the crowd knew of powered balloons, dirigibles and airships, having thrilled at the aeronautical adventures of 'Robur the Conqueror' aboard his Clipper of the Clouds thirteen years ago in the best-seller penned by my old Frankish friend, Jules Verne. The populace would not prove to be a problem. But the politicians would. And Wicko knew it.

As soon as he and Phoebe had entrusted Michael's corpse into the care of Dr. Phunn and his sister, Wicko was keen to get back underway.

"We need to get underway," he told Phoebe in no uncertain terms. She stared blankly. "Miss! Listen to me! We cannot stay here. We need to leave. Now!"

This was a new Wicko. Stern. Urgent. Implacable. Snapping her back into the real world. "Then you have to go without me." Phoebe's insistence was just as forceful.

"No! Miss! We need to fly to the theatre. You've got to alert the Professor while I conceal the Dodo! I don't have time to do the lot of it myself!"

"Wicko, I am staying with Michael!!"

Dr. Phunn saw the agonised frustration on the face of the dwarf.

"I have a solution," announced the oriental genius. "Mr. Spindleshanks."

Spindle, Dr. Phunn's painfully thin acrobatic associate, stepped forward and bowed.

"Thank you, to be kind enough to assist Mr. Smawl?"

Manswick Smawl. That was our dwarf's given name, so naturally we called him Wicko.

"Chriiist." Spindle's entire body stiffened. He was not best pleased. Wicko was hardly a firm favourite.

"Spindle," hissed Wu Hu, Dr. Phunn's wondrously beautiful sister.

Suitably persuaded, the skeletal funambulist whispered: "As you desire, Doctor. And Miss Wu Hu," while bowing so deeply his slender frame resembled a large hairpin.

The immediate problem pragmatically solved, Wicko nodded his thanks and scurried away, while Spindle somersaulted the short distance to the Dodo. Wicko sniffed as he watched. No doubt our dwarfish friend would have rewarded Spindle's showboating with a smack in the kisser with a spanner, just as he had once with that hideous, slobbering creature which turned out to be the local priest, Father Connor O'Connor. But

Wicko had neither time nor wrench to display his vexed irritation. Instead he clambered aboard and up into his Captain's seat, there at the business end of the Dodo's plush flight deck saloon. In a flurry of purpose, Wicko fired up the Aethyr generator, turned this and yanked on that to close the access door, all while easing the Dodo from the moist grass of Regent's Park and into the night sky. The diminutive aeronaut spun the helmswheel to the left, and started issuing his orders.

"Right, Spindle, this is what needs to be done. Here, never mind any of that looking outside business. Listen to what I'm saying."

Spindle was naturally mesmerised by the panoramic view through the five Window-Screens; the silhouetted skyline ahead, the rows of yellow dot lamp lights lining roadways three hundred feet below.

Inside, the eerie green glow from the array of clocks and dials bathing Wicko's face lent him an air of evil menace: "Right. I'm going to dive her down to the roof of the Theatre, close as I can, but I don't have time to land. So, I need you to jump down onto the roof. Are you up to that?"

"Chriiist!" said Spindle, his limbs stiffening again.

Wicko took Spindle's sharp features turning the colour of curdled milk to be a clear sign that he was: "You need to get inside the theatre. Never mind none of your burgling malarkey, there's a keyboard 'neath a cover flap by the Stage Door." Wicko frequently shifted his glance between Spindle and the Window-Screen as he spoke. "Using the keyboard, you need to type in the code which opens the Stage Door. The letters to type are: M A G I C." He spelt it out.

"Chriiist!"

"No. Not 'Christ'. 'Magic'. Though some might say it's one and the same thing. Magic. Tell me you've got that."

Spindle nodded.

"Then, listen to me, *then*, I need you to find the Professor. Though I reckon once you've got yourself inside he'll find you. I want you to forget the formalities, just tell him this." Wicko explained what to say.

"Chriiist! What does it mean?"

"He'll know. Best get yourself ready, me bony old friend. We are coming up on the theatre."

Spindle began stretching and bending, contorting his limbs into the most unimaginable positions as the Dodo tracked Church Street below, across the Market; then she came upon the junction with the Edgware Road where Wicko helmed a sharp left. At once the airship pitched to port. The welcome outline of the ornate twin cupolas atop the roof of the Metropolitan Theatre of Steam, Smoke and Mirrors hove into view. Wicko hauled back on the power, dropping the Dodo like a stomach-churning stone. A tug of the overhead lever slid open the access door. A shrill blast of cold, damp air exploded into the flight deck. Twenty feet. Fifteen. Ten feet. The wet, leaden flat roof swept along below. Spindle needed no prompting. He leapt, landed with a roll, was up on his feet, vaulting the ornate balustrade and scuttling down the back wall into White Horse Alley, all in one endless fluid action. It was a proper pity the Wicko saw none of it. Already he had punched the power and screamed the Dodo up and away toward the Marble Arch.

2.

Almost before the shouting began and the Brimstone billowed, Superintendent William Melville, head of the Metropolitan Police Special Branch, had heaved and hauled the Prince of Wales out of Westminster Abbey into his carriage and commanded the royal coachman to "Drive!". Melville pinned the strewn Royal to the back seat of the coach. A position with which Edward was not unfamiliar, although usually it was Mrs. Keppell or Mrs. Langtry doing the pinning.

Only when satisfied the coach was well clear of danger did Melville allow The Prince of Wales to restore his regal dignity.

"Fine work … from young Magister … back there, Melville," shouted the Prince, between deep nerve-settling draws on his cigar which, in the turmoil, he'd somehow managed to light. "My daught… Miss Le Breton? She is safe?"

"So far as I could see, sir." Melville ordered the coachman to steer for the Prince's residence, Marlborough House.

"Belay that," hollered Edward. "Steer to Pont Street!" He looked at Melville. "Mrs Langtry. She knows how to sustain one in circumstances most trying."

"Yes, she probably does," thought Melville.

With the Prince of Wales safely in the consoling arms of Lillie, Melville collared a Hansom to Arlington Place and the Prime Ministerial residence. Lord Salisbury much preferred the palatial luxury of his own Mayfair mansion to the muddle in that Downing Street cul-de-sac. Salisbury, too, was puffing furiously on a cigar as he paced up and down his dim-lit living room.

This had been the second outrage in a matter of weeks where the Prime Minister had escaped certain death, he complained, by being bundled without recourse to any decorum into his carriage. Such ignominy. And in public. *And* both assassinations had been foiled thanks, not to the police, but to Melville's consultants! Those two Music Hall magicians. Worse yet, one was an American, and if that wasn't shocking enough, the other was a girl! Of all the things! *And*, most recently, Magister and Le Breton had thwarted that attempt on the life of Her Majesty the Queen at Windsor Castle. (An account of this nail-biter can be found recorded in my paper, "The Windsor Curiosity".)

"How could we not know of such a thing," whined Salisbury, waving his cigar and showering the air with spittle and smuts of orange ash. His was a shrill voice, very much at odds with what you might expect from man of such a fulsome size.

"Indeed, Prime Minister," said Melville calmly. "Mercifully, His Majesty was unharmed. Nevertheless, the secrecy of the meeting was compromised, and without doubt we are possessed of a traitor in our midst."

"Not the plot to kill myself and His Majesty, Melville. We know there's a traitor among our ranks. I am talking about the flying machine, man. Did you see the flying machine?"

Melville took a pause. He knew where this was going. "It could hardly escape my attention, Prime Minister."

"And you watched the manner in which it soared aloft. The ease with which it took to the heavens!"

"Indeed."

"Then, sir, as the head of my Special Branch, I ask you this. How can tuppenny ha'penny Music Hall conjurers possibly possess such a vehicle when Her Majesty's forces do not?" Salisbury's face was disdainful even at the best of times. And now was certainly not the best of times.

"There is much in the life of Mr. Michael Magister and his associates that confounds us, Prime Minister. And now with his airship, it would seem he has surpassed all expectations."

"Ye Gods, man, it would seem he has! As we speak von Zeppelin beseeches the widow Schwarz for the patent of her husband's dirigible. The French are long advanced in the industry of mechanised flight. The armies of Europe must not be afforded such aeronautical advantage over Her Majesty's Empire. The nation needs Magister's airship, Melville. And you shall procure that vehicle for me."

"With respect, Prime Minister…"

"Do as I order, Superintendent," growled Salisbury, as best anyone could with a falsetto voice given to the dusty end of the keyboard. But those glaring sag-bag eyes left Melville in no doubt as to the Prime Minister's resolve. "I want that airship, Melville. Even if you must kill to get it."

3.

I was at my work bench in the Dungeon beneath the stage, trying to concentrate on my patent perpetual motion device which I was now convinced would work, if only I could get the damned thing started.

The red warning bulb on the brick wall before me glowed. Much relief. Wicko, Michael and Phoebe had returned safely from their annoying mission of mercy. In time for the late performance. Except that … they would descend from the roof aboard the Lift'n'Shift platform. The red bulb only signalled pedestrian access through the Stage Door. That was disturbing. More so when the bulb began a series of repeated flashes. Someone, other than my magicians, was at the Stage Door, tapping away at the entry keyboard and failing with the password not once, but twice. We were resigned to the occasional Phoebe worshipper brute-forcing his luck through the door, or to a hormonal Michael follower looking to sate her passion by gaining access to the theatre, but not while the drinking dens were still serving.

Perhaps it was a furious patron, demanding to know if the second show would proceed. Then the red light died. Splendid. The stage door Johnny or Jenny had given up and gone. Then the green lamp shone brightly. Ah. *That* was not quite so splendid. Whoever it was had not given up and gone at all. Instead, they'd happened on the correct entry code – and gained access to the theatre. I ran a gnarled finger along the various blunt, sharp and heavy work precision tools at my disposal. What would Wicko use? He was merciless. But I could be worse. I selected the axe.

Outside, in White Lion Alley, under the Stage Door light, Spindle had squinted at the keyboard and with one finger tapped in M A F U C to no charming effect, and then tried M A J I C. Clearly spelling had never been the strongest, nor most necessary skill amongst the acrobatic community. Give Spindle a safe and he could crack it in moments. But, you see, that was numbers. He was already jigging and jumping. Mercifully, before he started cursing and Chriiisting, Spindle hit success.

M A G I C.

The Stage Door hissed, unclicked, and swung inwards a tad. Spindle nudged it marginally wider with a cautious finger, waited, then slipped easily through the gap, from the airy light of the alley into the eerie darkness of the lobby. Feeling more at ease, the consummate burglar squinted his eyes to penetrate the murk. This was his world. Where he who could see could not be seen. Or something like that. Sadly, his comfort was somewhat short lived when the lamps of the lobby flickered, then warmed the lobby in a gentle sepia glow. Wicko's desk and chair, and the props trunk, the double swing-doors which led to the dressing room stairs.

Spindle jumped again when the Stage Door hissed and closed behind him, then jumped a darn sight higher when the lid of the props trunk hinged open and I emerged; hunched, wild-eyed and wielding an axe like a psychopathic killer from a tableau in Tussaud's Chamber of Horrors.

"CHRIISST!!"

"Spindle?" Yes, I knew him.

"Professor?! Don't kill me!!" He cringed and protected his head. "Chriiist!! No! I've brought a message! From the dwarf. He said to tell you – it's London Bridge!"

"What did you say?"

"It's London Bridge."

It had always been inevitable. Always. Nevertheless, my blood chilled.

4.

Phoebe peered at Michael's corpse through the porthole atop the Sarcophagus. His eyes were masked with goggles. The strange curative green light bathing his entire naked body. As it had with Lazarus. But this time, she realised, Dr. Phunn's remarkable machine flattered to deceive. For only now she noticed the fluid lines snaking into

Michael's arms and legs. Air, or gas, she had no idea what, breezed into the heavy metal tomb.

Phoebe felt a comforting hand squeeze her shoulder. "Patience," said Wu Hu.

Michael never saw the two beautiful faces looking down upon him. But in the deep void that is death, a single spark of life flashed through his mind. Like a lamp's splutter. Then another flash. And another. The images came. Faster. Brighter. Invading his vague and distant thoughts. Becoming clearer. The explosion. The falling. The memories. Swirling. Clearer.

Then colourful ... and so VIVID!

Michael's body tensed. Finally – he knew the answers.

He knew where he came from! And more importantly *how*!

He remembered it all!

Thank you for reading *The Windsor Curiosity.*

We hope you enjoyed reading *The Windsor Curiosity* and would consider leaving a review for the book or a rating. It means so much to authors and publishers to get feedback about our books, so we can improve them and keep delivering books you love. All of our books are professionally edited and proofread by our editorial team, however, occasionally a mistake might slip through. If you do find something, we hope that this would not spoil your enjoyment of the book but please make a note of it and send the details through to info@caffeinenights.com and we will amend it and ensure we give you something in return for your efforts.

Caffeine Nights Newsletter

If you would like to know more about the next Colin Edmonds novel or any of our other authors or books, please sign up for our free newsletter at www.caffeinenights.com/newsletter. Your email address and details are completely safe with us and never passed on or sold to anyone else and there is an unsubscribe link in every email should you choose you no longer want to receive our newsletter. All new newsletter subscribers can download a free eBook too.

We love social media and tweeting or posting on Facebook or putting a pic on Instagram is a great way to tell folks what you have enjoyed. You can follow us at:

Twitter: @caffeinenights

Facebook: CaffeineNights

Instagram: @caffeinenights

And if you share anything about our books we will share with our followers.

Printed in Great Britain
by Amazon